ABDO Publishing Company is the exclusive school and library distributor of Rabbit Ears Books.

Library bound edition 2005.

Copyright © 1995 Rabbit Ears Productions, Inc.,
Rowayton, Connecticut.

Library of Congress Cataloging-in-Publication Data

Metaxas, Eric.
  The story of Brer Rabbit and the wonderful tar baby / collected by Joel Chandler Harris ;
adapted by Eric Metaxas ; illustrated by Henrik Drescher.
       p. cm.
  "Rabbit Ears books."
  Summary: Relates how the wily Brer Rabbit outwits Brer Fox, who has set out to trap him.
  ISBN 1-59197-761-4
  [1. African Americans—Folklore. 2. Animals—Folklore. 3. Folklore—United States.] I.
Drescher, Henrik, ill. II. Harris, Joel Chandler, 1848-1908. Brer Rabbit and the wonderful
tar baby. III. Title.

PZ8.1.M518Br 2004
398.2—dc22
[E]

                                                                        2004045796

All Rabbit Ears books are reinforced library binding
and manufactured in the United States of America.

The Story of BRER Rabbit
and the wonderful Tar Baby

collected by
Joel Chandler Harris

adapted by
Eric Metaxas

illustrated by
Henrik Drescher

Rabbit Ears Books

Way, way back in the beginning of things, when this old world was just a baby, there lived a whole gathering of creatures—big ones, little ones, and every kind you can imagine, down at the edge of a great swamp.

Most of the time there was a considerable amount of peace, love, and understanding between them, and generally speaking they were about as neighborly as you can imagine—you see, back then, everything the brethren needed to get by with was right there amongst them, and if it happened that one of them couldn't locate what he needed, well, you can bet your Sunday shoes that one of his neighbors would have it, and they would work out a fair swap.

Of course every great once in a while—or maybe it was every now and then—I can't remember—if the day was just a little too long or the old round moon was just a little too round, some of these happy children would get to thinking, and that's how old man trouble got his start.

You see, sooner or later one or the other of the brethren would look around and somehow get to figuring out it was his neighbor who always got more than he did. Then he'd reckon how it was his neighbor who did less work than he did. Well, next thing you knew you'd have a genuine situation on your hand. And whenever there was a genuine situation, there'd be a fair-sized portion of scheming to go right alongside it, and the minute you got one of the brethren scheming a way to get the better of one of his fellow brethren you'd have a regular tornado of commotion, just as sure as there are bees in a buzzing hive.

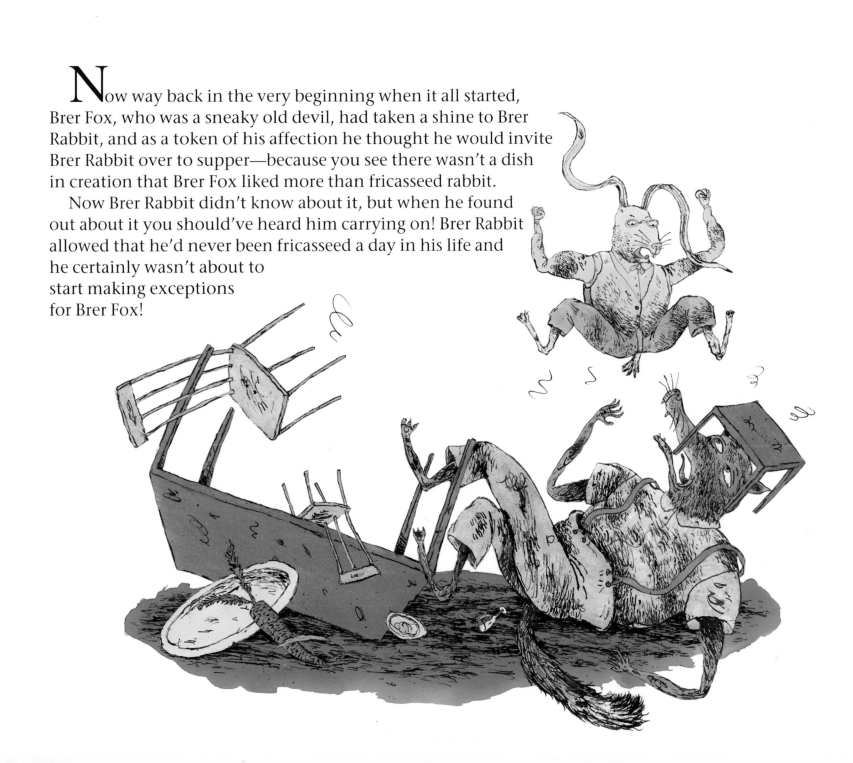

Now way back in the very beginning when it all started, Brer Fox, who was a sneaky old devil, had taken a shine to Brer Rabbit, and as a token of his affection he thought he would invite Brer Rabbit over to supper—because you see there wasn't a dish in creation that Brer Fox liked more than fricasseed rabbit.

Now Brer Rabbit didn't know about it, but when he found out about it you should've heard him carrying on! Brer Rabbit allowed that he'd never been fricasseed a day in his life and he certainly wasn't about to start making exceptions for Brer Fox!

But poor old Brer Fox confessed that he was mighty particular about what he ate, particularly when it came to fricasseed rabbit. As a matter of fact, his tastes tended toward one fricasseed rabbit in particular, and it was that fact in particular that particularly bothered Brer Rabbit!

Well, by and by Brer Rabbit got so mad at Brer Fox that pretty soon he figured out a way to get back at Brer Fox, and get back he did.

It seemed that for a while there all Brer Rabbit ever did was sass old Brer Fox. That Brer Rabbit hardly took the time out to eat, he was so busy sassin'. And it went on like that for so long that the creatures almost never talked about it anymore, because it was such an old story.

But sooner or later Brer Fox up and decided that he'd had about all he could take of Brer Rabbit's sass, and he figured out a clever plan whereby he'd get Brer Rabbit back once and for all.

So early one day Brer Fox went to work, and he got himself some tar. And he mixed it up with some turpentine and fixed himself up a contraption that he most appropriately called a Tar-Baby.

And he took the Tar-Baby and set her down by the side of the big road, and then he laid low in the bushes to see what was going to happen.

And he didn't have to wait too long either, because by and by Brer Rabbit came along, pacing down the road—lippity-clickity, lippity-clickity—just as light as the air—because he was so brought up by his own natural sassiness.

Now Brer Fox, he just laid low, and Brer Rabbit came prancing along until he spied the Tar-Baby, and the minute he saw it he fetched himself onto his hind legs in astonishment. But the Tar-Baby, she just sat there, and Brer Fox, he just laid low.

"Good morning!" said Brer Rabbit. "Mighty nice weather we been having this morning, wouldn't you say?"

But the Tar-Baby, she didn't say a thing, and Brer Fox, he just laid low.

"And how is your disposition situated, O lovely lady?" said Brer Rabbit.

Brer Fox winked his eye slowly, but the Tar-Baby, she didn't say a thing.

"Your shyness stirs my heart. Pray, lovely lady, honor me with a word…Well, how are you doing? Can you hear me? Because if you can't, I can holler louder."

But the Tar-Baby, she didn't say a thing, and Brer Fox, he just laid low.

"You stuck up, that's what you are! And I'm going to cure you of it, that's what I'm going to do!"

Brer Fox sort of chuckled to himself very quietly, but the Tar-Baby, she didn't say a thing.

"I'll teach you how to talk to respectable folks if it's my last act!" said Brer Rabbit. "If you don't take off that hat and say 'Howdy,' I'm gonna bust you wide open." But the Tar-Baby, she just stood there and Brer Fox, he just laid low.

And Brer Rabbit, he kept on romancin', and the Tar-Baby, she kept on saying nothing, until presently Brer Rabbit drew back his fist and blip, whacked the Tar-Baby right on the side of her head.

And that's where he broke the proverbial molasses jug. And his fist got stuck and he couldn't pull it loose—because the tar held him. But the Tar-Baby, she still just stood still and Brer Fox, he still just laid low.

"If you don't le'me go, I'll knock you sideways," said Brer Rabbit, and with that he fetched the Tar-Baby a swipe with his other hand—and that got stuck too! And the Tar-Baby, she didn't say a thing, and Brer Fox, he still laid low.

"Turn me loose before I kick the natural stuffing outta you," said Brer Rabbit. And the Tar-Baby, she didn't say a thing, she just held on. And still old Brer Fox laid just about as low as he could.

And then Brer Rabbit lost the use of his feet in the same way.

Brer Rabbit squealed out if the Tar-Baby didn't turn him loose that minute, he'd butt her crankside with his head. And then he butted and his head got stuck! And no sooner than that very minute Brer Fox sauntered forth from the bushes, looking just as innocent as one of your mother's mockingbirds.

"Well howdy, Brer Rabbit," said Brer Fox. "You look sort of stuck up this morning," and with that he rolled around on the ground and laughed and laughed until he couldn't laugh no more.

Now most thinkin' folks might a' supposed that right there would be the final and tragic end of poor old Brer Rabbit, because everybody and his brother knows that Brer Fox had been trying to catch Brer Rabbit for a mighty long time. But Brer Rabbit was an awful clever creature—he and his family were at the head of the gang when there was any trouble on hand and he wasn't about to resign himself to any stew pot just yet. So before you start making any calculations and weeping over Brer Rabbit, you just wait and see where it is he turns up.

Now when Brer Fox found Brer Rabbit mixed up with the Tar-Baby, he felt mighty good. And it was a long time before he could stop laughing and get back onto his feet. But by and by he gathered himself up and spoke.

"Well, I expect I got you this time, Brer Rabbit. It's possible I don't, but I expect I do. You been running round here sassing after me for a mighty long time, but I expect you come to the end of the row. You been cutting your capers and bouncing around this here neighborhood until you come to think you the boss of the whole shebang! And you always somewhere you've got no business at all. Who asked you to come and strike up a acquaintance with this here Tar-Baby? And who got you stuck where you are? Nobody in the round world. You just went and jammed yourself onto that Tar-Baby without any invitation whatsoever, and there you are and there you'll stay until I fix up a brush pile and fire it up, because I'm going barbecue you this very day."

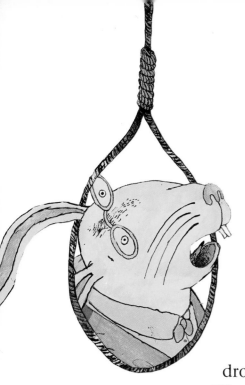

Then Brer Rabbit spoke mighty humble. "I don't care what you do with me, Brer Fox," he said, "as long as you don't fling me into that briar patch yonder. You can roast me just as long as you please, but whatever you do, Brer Fox, please don't fling me into that briar patch."

"It's so much trouble to kindle a fire," said Brer Fox, rubbing his jaw, "that I expect maybe I'll just have to hang you."

"You can hang me just as high as you please, Brer Fox," said Brer Rabbit. "You can hang me upside down and you can hang me sideways, but for the Lord's sake, Brer Fox, please don't fling me into that briar patch yonder."

"Well, I haven't got any string to speak of, so I…I expect I'll just have to drown you."

"You can drown me just as deep as you please, Brer Fox," said Brer Rabbit, "and you can drown me once or you can drown me nine times, but whatever you do, Brer Fox, please don't fling me into that briar patch yonder."

"Shucks. Seeing how there isn't any water near here," said Brer Fox, "I expect I'll just have to skin you."

"You can skin me, Brer Fox, you can snatch out my eyeballs, you can tear my ears out by the roots, and you can cut off my legs—but please, Brer Fox, whatever you do, for the Lord's own sake, please don't fling me into that briar patch yonder."

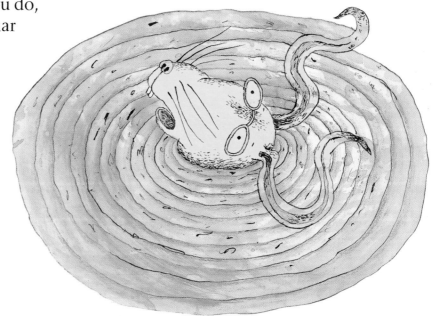

But because Brer Fox wanted to hurt Brer Rabbit just about as much as he could, he knew there was only one thing to do, and so he picked him up by the hind legs and slung him right into the middle of the briar patch.

Now there was a considerable amount of commotion where Brer Rabbit struck the bushes, and old Brer Fox sort of hung around to see what was going to happen. And by and by he heard somebody calling him, and way, way up on the hill he saw Brer Rabbit sitting cross-legged on a chinkapin log, combing the pitch out of his hair with a chip.

And that's when Brer Fox knew he'd been had. Brer Rabbit was mighty pleased to fling back some of his well-known sass, and he hollered out: "Bred and born in a briar patch, Brer Fox—bred and born in a briar patch!" And with that he skipped away just as lively as a cricket in the embers.